The Berenstain Bears
and the
BLAME GAME

When cubs are at play,
it's always the same.
Accidents happen.
Who's to blame?

A First Time Book®

The Berenstain Bears and the

BLAME GAME

Stan & Jan Berenstain

Random House 🏠 New York

Copyright © 1997 by Berenstain Enterprises, Inc. All rights reserved under International and Pan-American Copyright Conventions. Published in the United States by Random House, Inc., New York, and simultaneously in Canada by Random House of Canada Limited, Toronto.
http://www.randomhouse.com/
Library of Congress Cataloging-in-Publication Data
Berenstain, Stan, 1923– The Berenstain Bears and the blame game / Stan & Jan Berenstain.
p. cm. — (First time books)
SUMMARY: Members of the Bear family try to solve their problems without playing the blame game of arguing over who is responsible for every disaster.
ISBN 0-679-88743-1 (trade). — ISBN 0-679-98743-6 (lib. bdg.)
[1. Responsibility—Fiction. 2. Behavior—Fiction. 3. Bears—Fiction.]
I. Berenstain, Jan, 1923– . First time books. PZ7.B4483Bebd 1997 [E]—dc21 97-6750
Printed in the United States of America 10 9 8 7 6 5 4 3 2 1

You all know the Bear family that lives in the big tree house down a sunny dirt road deep in Bear Country. And, of course, you know Mama Bear—warm, friendly Mama Bear, from whom seldom is heard a discouraging word.

But lately, Mama hadn't been all that friendly. Her smile was gone and she was feeling *very* discouraged. Why? Because life in the big tree house had turned into one long, miserable, never-ending blame game.

Cries of "He started it!" "No, she started it!" and "It was her fault!" "No, it was his fault!" filled the air from day to night.

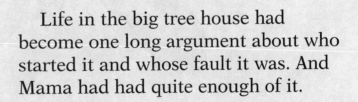

IT WAS HER FAULT!

NO, IT WAS HIS FAULT!

HER FAULT!

HIS FAULT!

Life in the big tree house had become one long argument about who started it and whose fault it was. And Mama had had quite enough of it.

So when she heard the sounds of breaking glass and spilling water, she rushed into the living room. There she found a mess of broken glass, spilled water, and a scatter of roses on the floor.

Standing over the mess were Brother and Sister Bear. They were pointing at each other and shouting, "It was her fault!" "No, it was *his* fault!" over and over again.

Mama looked at the mess. She had cut those roses and put them in a vase with water just that morning.

She looked at Brother and Sister, who were still pointing and shouting at each other.

It was time to put a stop to the blame game. Mama decided to put her foot down—*hard*. So hard it shook the room.

"Enough of this blame game!" she shouted. "I want to know who really started it, and I want to know right now!"

Well, it was like peeling back the layers of an onion. It was enough to make you cry. Mama might have if she hadn't been so angry. And the more Brother and Sister pointed and shouted, the angrier Mama got.

"He knocked it over!" cried Sister. "He made the mess!"

"But that was only because she was trying to poke me in the ribs!" shouted Brother.

"I was *not* trying to poke him," protested Sister. "I was just trying to tickle him because he tickled me this morning."

"But that was because
she tickled me last night."

"But that was because he put
a rubber snake on my bed."

SQUEAK!

"But that was because she put
a squeaky toy on my chair and it
squeaked when I sat down."

And so it went. But, but, but. Because, because, because. Mama understood that she wasn't getting to the bottom of anything. But she *was* getting to the end of her patience. Her head was awhirl with "buts," "becauses," rubber snakes, squeaky toys, broken glass, spilled water, and scattered roses.

"ENOUGH!" she shouted.

"Enough of what?" asked Papa Bear.

He had been fixing up the downstairs bay window and heard the shouting. "From what I've heard," he said, looking at the mess on the floor, "there's more than enough blame to go around. So instead of playing the blame game, why don't we just go to work and solve the problem?"

"Let's deal with the broken glass for starters. Brother, you fetch the dustpan and broom. Sister, you bring the paper towels from the kitchen."

Papa quickly swept the bigger pieces
of broken glass into the dustpan.

"What about the water and the roses and
the little pieces of broken glass?" asked Sister.

"Mama," said Papa, "will you please pick up the roses? But look out for thorns and broken glass."

Then he laid paper towels on the whole wet mess.

He swept what was left
into the dustpan.

Mama put the roses
into another vase.

Good for Papa! He had put a stop to the blame game!

Papa went back to his workshop. The cubs went out to play.

But while Papa was putting away his paint and putty, *he* heard the sound of breaking glass.

He rushed outside. The bay window he had just painted and puttied was broken! There stood Brother and Sister, pointing at each other. Sister had a bat. Brother had a glove. There was a baseball in the grass among pieces of broken glass.

Papa bit his lip, counted to ten, took a deep breath...

...and did a very good imitation of a volcano.

"It seems to me," said Mama, who had heard the crash, "that instead of shouting and pointing fingers, we should get to work and solve the problem."

And that's what they did. They picked up the glass and went to work. It took some doing, but after a while the window was painted and puttied as good as new.

"Of course, there *are* times," said Papa,
"when somebody really *is* to blame for
something. But most of the time, it's
important to remember there's usually
enough blame to go around."